GUNDI HERGET   NIKOLAI RENGER

ARNOLD
THE
BRAVE

PETER PAUPER PRESS, INC.
White Plains, New York

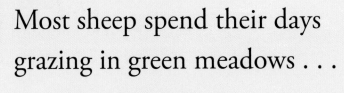

Most sheep spend their days
grazing in green meadows . . .

"BAAAA"

. . . all except Arnold. He's not like most sheep.

Arnold runs . . .

does squats . . .

pull-ups . . .

push-ups . . .

and even boxes.

As far as Arnold is concerned, any old sheep can graze.
But like we said, Arnold is not like any old sheep.

"I am a Super Sheep!" says Arnold.

But that's not what the other sheep think.
They just don't get Arnold.

"HUSH, HUSH!
DON'T RUSH!"

"Just you wait," says Arnold. "One day those sheep will see that I AM a Super Sheep!"

Only Milo the mole recognizes Arnold's greatness.

Milo is Arnold's best friend, and biggest fan— his *only* fan, to be exact.

"WOW, ARNOLD!"

Milo helps Arnold with his training—

just a little bit.

After all, a Super Sheep
never needs much help.

Well, almost never.

One day Landon the lookout sheep came running and bleated in fear, "The wolf is coming! The wolf is coming!"

"BAAAA!"

The sheep began to panic.

"The wolf! The wolf!"

"What will we do?" they yelled.

"We'll run away!" some shouted.

"We'll hide!" said others.

"We'll call for the sheepdog!"

But then a lone voice bellowed from the flock,

"No! I will *fight* the wolf!"

The entire meadow went silent . . .

. . . and then erupted into laughter.

"*Fight* the wolf?" they asked.
"Are you crazy, Arnold?
You need to hide like the rest
of us, you silly."

"HAHA"

"HEEE"

"HAHAHA"

"No I don't," said Arnold boldly.

"HAAHAA..."

"I've been training for this moment my whole life."

All of the sheep went into hiding . . .

. . . all except Arnold.

He firmly planted his hooves,
stood in the middle of the meadow—
forelegs up and ready for battle.

His friend Milo squeaked,
"I can't watch!" and took off his glasses.

"Put 'em up, Wolf! Put 'em up!" demanded Arnold.
"I'm not scared of you!"

The wolf stopped in his tracks.
He couldn't believe his eyes.
A sheep standing its ground?
Not running away? Not hiding? Not calling for the sheepdog?

(Meanwhile, Milo clung to his molehill in fear.)

"BAAAA!"

The wolf had never seen a sheep like Arnold.

He watched him prance around, throwing punches in the air, shouting, "You won't get me, Wolf! I'm a Super Sheep!"

"HAHAAA"

The wolf started to laugh. And laugh . . . and laugh. "I'll clobber you!" shouted Arnold.

The wolf was laughing so hard, he didn't see
what was happening. (Neither did Arnold.)

But Arnold's best friend Milo was busy
providing a little help—just a little bit.

After all, a Super Sheep never needs much help anyway.

Well, almost never.

"Come closer if you dare!" taunted Arnold.

And so the wolf . . .

Well, sort of.

BAM! The wolf fell to the ground with a thud!

"Ah-ha!" declared Arnold.
"I, Arnold the Super Sheep, have defeated the
mighty wolf with my strength and prowess!"

"Bravo!" yelled Milo. "Bravo!"

The sheep were astonished.
Arnold had defeated the wolf—
just like he said!

"WAY TO GO, ARNOLD!"

"BRAVO!"

"Job well done!" said lookout Landon.
"You are the bravest of the flock—a true hero!"

As a big thank you, the sheep gave Arnold a
very special present.

"SPLENDID,
ARNOLD!"

Because every Superhero needs a cape!

From that day forward, while all the other sheep grazed safely in the meadow, Arnold—assisted by Milo—kept close watch.

For he was no ordinary sheep. He WAS the Great Defender of his flock—Arnold the Brave, Super Sheep.

First published in the United States by Peter Pauper Press, Inc.
Originally published in Germany as *Arnold, Retter der Schafheit* by Magellan GmbH & Co. KG.
Copyright © 2017 Magellan GmbH & Co. KG, Bamberg, Germany
English translation copyright © 2018 by Peter Pauper Press, Inc.
Translation by Ann Garlid

Published by Peter Pauper Press, Inc.
202 Mamaroneck Avenue
White Plains, New York 10601 USA

Published in the United Kingdom and Europe by Peter Pauper Press, Inc.
c/o White Pebble International
Unit 2, Plot 11 Terminus Rd.
Chichester, West Sussex PO19 8TX, UK

Library of Congress Cataloging-in-Publication Data Available

ISBN 978-1-4413-2650-8
Manufactured for Peter Pauper Press, Inc.
Printed in Hong Kong

7 6 5 4 3 2 1

Visit us at www.peterpauper.com